D1503085

Delicious English
CARAMEL TREE

www.carameltree.com

Sarah Snow - Star of the Show!

CARAMEL TREE

Chapter 1

The List

Sarah saw the list as soon as she opened the gym doors. She walked across the gym floor quickly, trying not to look like she was in a hurry. She stopped in front of the piece of yellow paper taped to the wall outside Mr. Walker's office door. The soccer team list was short – there were only 16 names written in purple ink. She read through the names once. Her bottom lip

started to tremble. Starting at the top, she slowly read through the list a second time. Her brown eyes filled with big tears. Sarah bit her bottom lip to try and keep the tears inside.

"Did you make the team?" a familiar voice asked.

Sarah wiped her eyes, looked at her feet and shook her head.

"Oh, too bad," Wendy said. "I really wanted you to be on the soccer team." Before Sarah could respond, she was pushed out of the way by other girls. They all wanted to read the list.

"Yes, I made it!" shouted Ashley.

"Awesome – we both made it!" said Marita.

"Our team will be so much fun!" Wendy said, hugging her friends.

Sarah walked quietly back through the gym doors. She kept her eyes on the green tile floor in front of her. "I will not cry; I will not cry..." she told herself. Somehow, she made it to her locker, found the books she needed, and went to her classroom. She had tried so hard to make the soccer team, and she had played really well in the final try-out. She had almost scored, twice. Why hadn't she made it?

All day, soccer was the only thing anybody could talk about. A few girls told Sarah they were sorry she hadn't made the team. Some of them even said it wasn't fair.

"Ashley only made it because she is Mr. Walker's daughter," Wendy said. "She runs like a turtle."

Sarah smiled weakly. "But she can play goalie," she said. "All I can do is run fast."

"At least you're a good team player, though," Wendy said. "Ashley always gets mad at us if we don't stop the other team from scoring on her. She always complains about everything."

Sarah shrugged. "It's not the end of the world," she said. "At least you made the team." Even though she was sad that she wasn't chosen to be on the soccer team, Sarah was happy for her friend, Wendy.

At the end of the day, Sarah walked by the gym on her way to the bus. The soccer players were gathered outside Mr. Walker's office. They were all talking and laughing excitedly as he passed out the uniforms, and they got dressed for their first practice. Wendy waved when she saw Sarah standing outside the door. Sarah waved back, then turned and walked outside. She took in a big breath of the cool, fall air and tried not to cry.

She felt a little better after she had found a seat on the bus. The new girl, Kaitlin, sat down beside her. She had just moved to Kingston from the West Coast, and she was twelve, a year older than Sarah.

"How was your day?" Kaitlin asked.

"Not very good," Sarah answered. "Horrible, in fact."

"Mine, too," Kaitlin said. "I wanted to be on the soccer team, but I haven't been at this school long enough."

"I didn't make the team, either," Sarah said.

"Want to come over to my house after school some day?" Kaitlin asked.

Sarah smiled. "I'll have lots of free time, now that I won't be playing soccer. But today's my voice lesson.

How about tomorrow?"

"I take ballet on Wednesdays," Kaitlin said. "Maybe Thursday?"

Sarah hesitated. She knew Thursday was the girls' first soccer game. She really should go watch since most of her friends were on the team. *'I'm*

not even sure I like soccer,' Sarah thought to herself. She picked up her backpack and grinned at Kaitlin. "Sure," she said. "Thursday would be perfect. See you at school tomorrow!"

Sarah smiled as she saw her dog, Bailey, waiting for her outside the front door. She bent down to scratch her ears. "Hey, girl. How was your day? Boring as usual?"

Bailey wagged her tail and rolled over to have her stomach patted.

"Let's watch some TV," Sarah said. She tried not to think about the other girls at the soccer practice as she curled up with Bailey and scratched the little dog's floppy ears. "You're so lucky, Bailey. You don't have to worry about making teams, or friends, or being popular. I wish I was a dog."

Bailey woofed and rested her head on Sarah's legs.

Chapter 2

Another Try-Out

Sarah's mom looked up from the newspaper as Sarah came down the stairs the next morning. "Good morning, sweetie. How did you sleep?"

"Okay," Sarah said. "At least I didn't have any nightmares about not making the soccer team."

Her mother laughed. "You'll find something else to do, I'm sure. I see The Grand Theater is having open auditions for their Christmas musical this year. Are you interested in auditioning?"

Sarah looked over her mother's shoulder at the newspaper. "Girls between the ages of 10 and 15 – do you know how many girls will try out for that?"

"But you have a sweet voice, Sarah. Remember how much fun you had in the school musical last year?" Mrs. Snow said.

Sarah smiled. "It was fun, pretending to be somebody else. I suppose I could try. Will you make me an appointment? I could go after school."

"I'll give them a call today," her mother said. "Now, what do you want for breakfast? Toast or Cereal?"

When Sarah got to school, several girls were gathered around a red notice on the bulletin board. She could read the headline as she approached: "AUDITIONS."

'Oh, great. Now every girl in the school will try out. I hate try-outs!' Sarah thought.

"Hey, Sarah. Are you trying out for the musical?" Wendy called out as she saw Sarah at the back of the crowd. "You were awesome in the school musical last year."

Sarah felt guilty and smiled nervously. "I don't think so," she said. "I'm pretty busy with school and helping Mom with Bailey and the house. I don't think I have time."

Sarah didn't even blush as she told the white lie. It was clear that she was a good actress. Sarah felt she had to tell the white lie because she didn't want the other girls to know in case she didn't get the part.

As Wendy and Sarah stood chatting, Ashley came around the corner. "I'm sure I'll get a part. My dad says I'm a natural actress," she said. "The actors at The Grand Theater even get paid. It's a professional acting job. When I become a famous actress, I'll be able to say this was my first paid acting job."

"Too bad Ashley doesn't have much confidence," Wendy whispered to Sarah as they walked down the hall.

Sarah laughed. "Sometimes, I wish I had some of her confidence."

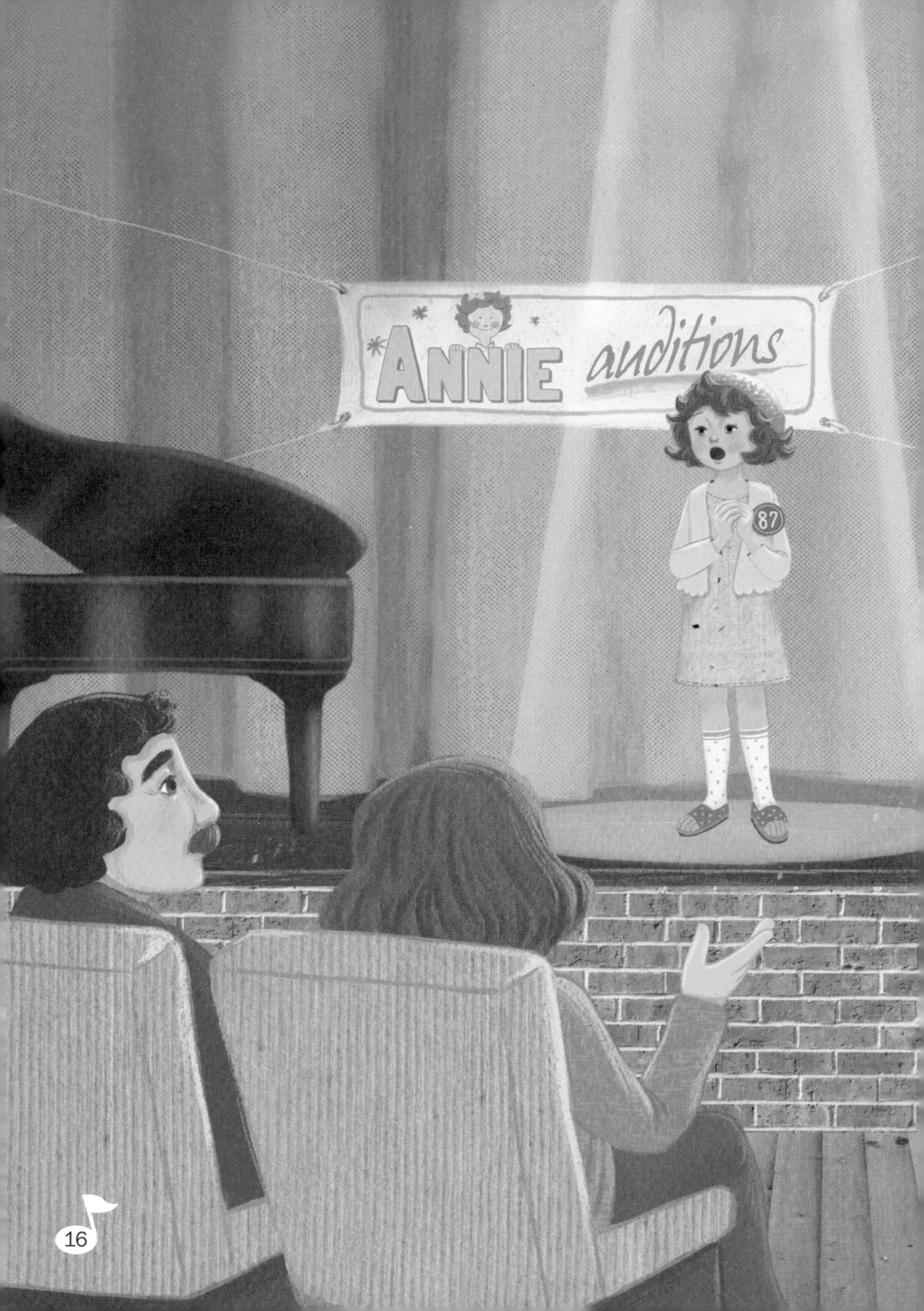
ANNIE auditions
87

After dinner, Sarah and her mom drove downtown. The theater was empty except for the piano player and three people sitting at the front of the theater. Sarah's was the last appointment of the day, and the director, Cameron Jacobs, looked very tired and frustrated. He smiled weakly at Sarah as she took her place on the stage. "You're number 87," he said. "Hopefully that's your lucky number."

Sarah smiled and nodded to the man at the piano when she was ready. She took a deep breath, cleared her throat and began to sing. Mr. Jacobs sat up straight, and his assistant and the choreographer looked at each other in wonder. Sarah could see the three of them whispering to each other as she sang.

When she finished, Mr. Jacobs got up and handed her a few pages from the script. "Start at the bottom of page 3. I'll read the other parts, and I'd like you to read the part of Annie," he said.

Sarah tried to imagine what it would feel like to be a little girl without parents. She looked at her mom sitting at the back of the theater. Mom pointed both her thumbs up in the air when she saw Sarah looking at her. Sarah imagined how horrible it would be not to have a mother. She already knew what it felt like not to have a father. Her dad had died when she was seven. As she read the lines, real tears came to her eyes, and she knew the director could hear the sadness in her shaky voice as well.

Sarah finished singing to the sound of applause. Mr. Jacobs stood up and beamed at Sarah. "You, my dear, have just made my day a whole lot brighter. Do you dance as well as you sing?"

Sarah blushed. "Well, I have been taking ballet and jazz since I was five."

"Would you mind taking your hat off?" the director asked. "We need a certain look for this character."

"Oh, sure...sorry." Sarah yanked off her hat and tried to flatten the red curls that came bouncing out as she set them free.

Mr. Jacobs looked at his assistant and the choreographer and nodded. "Perfect. Thank you for coming in, Sarah Snow. We'll be in touch within the next few days."

That night, Sarah had trouble getting to sleep. The audition had been so much fun – imagine if she got a chance to work as a real actress! She pictured Ashley's

face when she heard the news. Sarah looked out her bedroom window and saw one bright star, twinkling in the night sky. "Wish I may, wish I might, have the wish, I wish tonight..."

Chapter 3

Little Orphan Annie

The next morning, when Sarah arrived at school, she heard Ashley bragging to Wendy and the other soccer players.

"The director said I had the most beautiful voice he had ever heard from an eleven-year-old," Ashley said.

"Really? I heard there were almost 100 girls who auditioned yesterday," Wendy said.

"I'm almost certain I'll get the lead role. The director had tears in his eyes when I read some of Annie's lines." Ashley flipped her straight black hair back over her shoulder. "I can't wait to look for the perfect curly, red wig. I'd be a gorgeous redhead, don't you think?"

"I don't know. Black seems like a good color for you," Wendy said.

Sarah pretended to be busy getting her books out of her locker, so Ashley and the other girls wouldn't talk to her.

"Are you coming to our game on Thursday?" Wendy asked Sarah.

"Sorry. I'd really like to, but I have other plans," Sarah answered.

When Sarah returned from Kaitlin's house at dinnertime on Thursday, her mom handed her a piece of paper. "Oh, somebody left a message for you this morning while I was at work."

Sarah read the message out loud. "Please call Cameron Jacobs at The Grand Theater as soon as possible."

Sarah squealed and gave her mom a big hug. "He did seem to like me, didn't he?"

Mrs. Snow nodded. "I had a very good feeling after your audition. Well, what are you waiting for? Call him!"

Sarah took the cordless phone to her bedroom. Her hand was shaking as she punched in the telephone number of the theater. After she finished speaking with Mr. Jacobs, she lay back on the bed, curled up around Bailey and cried.

Her mom knocked gently on the door, then opened it. "Oh, sweetie. I'm sorry," she said.

Sarah sat up and wiped away her tears. "No – I'm crying because I'm happy. You're looking at Little Orphan Annie!"

"Good for you! You'll be the best Annie ever." Mrs. Snow kissed Sarah on the forehead. "I'm so proud of you, Sarah."

"But, Mom – let's not tell anybody. Okay?" Sarah said. "I mean... just in case it doesn't work out or something. Can this be our secret? I'm only going to tell Kaitlin because she doesn't know any of the other girls."

Mrs. Snow looked puzzled, but she nodded her head. "Sure, if that's what you want. But I did want to at least tell Ashley Walker's mother. She was bragging at work today about how well Ashley did at her audition."

"Maybe she'll get to be one of the other orphans,"

Sarah said. "She is a good singer. I have to admit that."

The next morning, a huge group of girls huddled around Ashley's locker. She seemed to be writing on their binders.

"Sign mine, Ashley," called Marita.

"Here, mine too!" echoed other girls.

Wendy leaned against Sarah's locker. "Ashley got the role of Tessie in the musical. Those

silly girls are all asking for her autograph, like she's a movie star or something."

Sarah smiled. "Good for her. I'm sure she'll be a perfect Tessie. Isn't she the one who is always complaining and bragging?"

Wendy laughed. "Maybe you're right. That would be a perfect role for her."

Ashley stopped Sarah and Kaitlin in the courtyard at recess. "Aren't you going to congratulate me, Sarah?"

Sarah rolled her eyes and said, "Sure. You'll be a perfect Tessie."

"Sorry, you didn't get a part," Ashley said. "Maybe next time. I'm going to get paid $200 a week, even during the weeks we're rehearsing."

"That's awesome," Sarah said. "Have fun!" Sarah turned to Kaitlin. "She'll be surprised to see me at the first rehearsal," she said.

Kaitlin laughed. "Thanks for getting me tickets for opening night. My Uncle Richard will be visiting us then, and I'm going to bring him with me."

At lunchtime, Sarah and Kaitlin took their lunches outside to eat at one of the picnic tables. They were just packing up their lunchboxes when they heard someone screaming and crying. People left their lunches, jumped up and ran in the direction of the noise.

Chapter 4

Broken Leg

Ashley lay on the ground in the middle of a huge crowd of kids. She was sobbing loudly, and her right leg was bent at a very strange angle. Her dad, Mr. Walker, bent over her with the fi rst aid kit from the gym. Within a few minutes, they heard the sounds of sirens approaching. Two paramedics jumped out of the ambulance, lifted Ashley onto a stretcher, and raced off in the direction of the hospital with the sirens blaring.

"What happened? Did anybody see what happened?" Principal Shields and several teachers walked through the crowd, trying to find any students who had seen the accident. "Did someone push her?"

"It looked like she was trying to fly," Marita said. "She was up on that wooden bridge, singing and twirling around. Then she just stepped off the edge and crashed to the ground."

"She must have been putting on a show for her fans," Kaitlin said. "That bridge between the playground equipment does look like a stage."

"I hope she'll be all right," Sarah said. "I think rehearsals for the musical start next week."

"How do you know?" Wendy said.

Sarah shrugged. "Well, the show opens in a month. I suppose they would need at least three weeks to rehearse."

"Maybe you could take her place," Wendy said. "You'd be much better than Ashley. Did you get invited to her birthday party?"

Sarah shook her head. "She probably only invited the girls on the soccer team."

"Her invitation said the party would be at an exciting surprise location. Probably the bowling alley or maybe the swimming pool. Some surprise that will be." Wendy laughed. "Do you want to come over on Saturday?"

"Um...I think I'm busy on Saturday," Sarah said. "Mom said something about an appointment in the city."

"Okay. Maybe we can hang out together next week sometime." Wendy started to walk away. "Give me a call if you're bored."

'I don't think I'll have much time to be bored, not for a few months,' Sarah thought to herself. She still couldn't believe she was going to be Annie. The thought of hundreds of people watching her on stage made her a little nervous. But, she couldn't wait for rehearsals to start! Still, it would have been nice to get invited to Ashley's birthday. Her parties were always more exciting than all the other girls' parties.

Chapter 5

Last-Minute Invitation

The three weeks of rehearsals flew by. Sarah only missed one day of school, but she was tired a lot of the time. She went directly to the theater in the city every day after school except Mondays.

"Hurry, Sarah. You don't want to be late for the dress rehearsal." Mrs. Snow looked at her watch as she stood at the bottom of the stairs.

"I was just looking over my script one more time," Sarah said. "How do I look?" She had put a flowered plastic shower cap on over her curls to keep them from getting messed up in the wind.

"Like a star!" her mom said. "Let's go. I'm very excited that Mr. Jacobs invited me to sit in on the dress rehearsal. You've been rehearsing for three weeks, and I haven't even seen one minute of the show."

"Mom, you know that's because some parents have tried to get too involved in other shows," Sarah said. She opened the car door and put her bag in the back. "Plus, you've helped me practice all my lines – you probably know them as well as I do."

"I know. I'm not complaining. What will you do with all the money you're earning – have you decided?" asked Mrs. Snow.

Sarah shook her head. "I think I'd like to go to theater school in the city this summer – Mr. Jacobs said I would have no problem getting in, but it's very expensive."

"I'm so proud of you, Sarah. You could stay with Aunt Cathy in the city. She'd love to have you visit her for a couple of weeks."

"The other girls have all been talking about buying tickets to see *Annie.* I hope they won't be mad that I kept it a secret when they see me on stage," Sarah said. She paused for a moment then added, "I still feel awful that Ashley won't get to be in the show. Her leg will be in the cast for at least two more weeks."

"I think she's getting lots of attention for her broken leg," Mrs. Snow said. "Her mother said the other kids are constantly helping her carry her bag and get to her classes. Poor girl, it must be difficult for her with the broken leg."

"She's having her birthday party this weekend, too. Wendy said Ashley's not telling anybody where the party will be. It's going to be a surprise," Sarah said. "I couldn't have gone even if she had invited me."

"You'll be too busy being a star! As they say in theater, break a leg! But, I mean good luck – don't you dare break a real leg! You've worked too hard to miss opening night!" Mrs. Snow gave Sarah a big hug. "Your dad would have been so proud of you, Sarah."

"I wish he could be here," Sarah said. "I still miss him."

"Me, too," Mrs. Snow said. "Remember what a beautiful singing voice he had?"

Sarah nodded, and then looked at the clock. "It's 3 o'clock – I'm late! Love you, Mom. See you after the show!" Sarah disappeared inside the actors' entrance door.

Other than a few people forgetting a few lines, the dress rehearsal went very well. When they got home at 11:00 o'clock, Sarah fell into bed exhausted.

The next morning, the telephone rang at 8:00 o'clock. "It's for you, Sarah," Mrs. Snow called up the stairs.

"Hello?" Sarah said sleepily.

"Hey, Sarah. It's Ashley. Marita is sick and can't come to my party tonight. You can come if you want to – we have room for one more girl."

"Uh – thanks, Ashley. But, I'm busy tonight. Have fun, though, and happy birthday," Sarah said.

"Fine – we're doing something extra special," Ashley said. "But if you're too busy for your friends, then that's just fine." She hung up without saying goodbye.

Sarah told her mother about the conversation. Mrs. Snow smiled. "That's a shame that she called you so late. I guess you won't be able to go but never mind."

Sarah smiled. "Ashley would be so surprised if she knew what I was really doing tonight."

"Everybody in town will know once it's in the newspapers next week," Mrs. Snow said.

Chapter 6

Sarah Snow, Star of the Show!

Sarah walked nervously around the green room at the back of the theater on opening night. Everyone performing was nervous, too. The other girls were giggling and trying to make each other relax. Mr. Jacobs called Sarah aside.

"How are you doing, Annie?" he asked. He put one arm around her shoulders.

Sarah tried to smile. "Okay," she said. "I'll be fine once I get on stage, but right now I'm scared. There are a lot of people out there; people who paid a lot of money to see the show. Last year, in our school show, there were only 100 people at each performance."

"The show tonight is sold out, and all 500 people are going to think you're wonderful," Mr. Jacobs said. "Just be Annie – forget about being Sarah Snow, just for a couple of hours. The audience will love you."

From behind the curtain, Sarah heard the audience get very quiet as the orchestra started. She took several deep breaths, and let them out slowly, counting to ten each time. She took her place on stage with the other girls and waited for the curtain to open. She whispered to herself just to make sure her voice was working. The theater lights went down, and the curtain whooshed open.

Sarah didn't look out at the audience until just before her first song. She got in position at the front of the stage, and was just about to open her mouth, when she looked down at the people sitting in the front row. She couldn't see very many faces because of the spotlights, but she did see Ashley Walker and her parents. Ashley was sitting in an aisle seat, and her broken leg was sticking out into the aisle. Her mouth hung wide open as she stared at Sarah. The other soccer players smiled and waved at Sarah. Ashley looked like she was about to cry.

Sarah looked away quickly and started to sing. She forgot about Ashley, she forgot about the soccer team and her life in Kingston. She was Little Orphan Annie, a lonely little girl looking for a loving family. Before she knew it, the show was over and she lined up with the other actors backstage, as they got ready to take their bows.

When it was her turn, Sarah ran to center stage, lifted the hem of her red dress and curtsied, then hurried back to join the other actors. Everyone in the crowd stood up at once. They yelled and whistled and clapped for a very long time. Some of the adults pushed Sarah forward again. "They're clapping for you," one of them whispered. Sarah took another bow, and the curtains closed.

She and the other performers went to the lobby after the show. The soccer players were waiting for her. They made a big circle around Sarah and chanted her name as they held out their programs for her to sign. Sarah blushed.

"You were awesome!" Wendy said. "And you're very good at keeping secrets, too!"

"Thanks – I'm sorry I kept it a secret," Sarah said. "I was just worried it might not work out."

"That was an awesome surprise," Wendy said. "I don't think Ashley will ever forget this birthday!" she whispered.

"You were pretty good," Ashley said, coming up behind them. "The girl who took my place playing Tessie wasn't very good, though."

Sarah smiled at Ashley. She was surprised to get a compliment from her.

Sarah stopped to sign a few other autographs. She saw her mom and Kaitlin standing with a handsome stranger in a corner. He was dressed in a very expensive-looking suit, and he had fancy glasses. He looked a little familiar. Sarah made her way through the crowd and gave her mom an extra big hug. "Thanks, Mom. I couldn't have done it without you," she said.

"I am so very proud of you, Sarah," her mom said.

"You were so good," Kaitlin said, giving her a hug. "This is my Uncle Richard. He's visiting from the West Coast."

The tall man reached out to shake Sarah's hand. "Richard Duncan – I'm very pleased to meet you, Sarah. You are an extremely talented young lady."

Sarah's mouth dropped open as she shook his hand. "THE Richard Duncan?" she said. "The Film Director?" Out of the corner of her eye, Sarah saw Ashley stop talking to her friends. She turned to stare at Sarah and Richard Duncan and moved closer.

Mr. Duncan smiled. "Yes. I had a few days off, and Kaitlin invited me to see the show. I'm looking for a young actress for my next film. Would you be interested in spending the summer in Hollywood?"

Sarah gasped and put both hands over her mouth. She looked at her mom.

"I think she's saying yes," Mrs. Snow said. "Right, Sarah?"

Sarah nodded her head. "Oh, yes. I was planning to go to theater school, but working with you would be so much better! Your movies are the best!"

"I'm glad you enjoy them," Mr. Duncan said.

"Are you really Richard Duncan?" Wendy asked. "THE Richard Duncan, famous Hollywood director?"

Richard smiled and nodded again.

"Let's go, girls," Ashley said loudly. "We're going to The Sweet Shop – they made a triple-layer chocolate fudge cake for my birthday."

"Wait a minute," Wendy said. "Didn't you hear him say he is Richard Duncan? Will you sign my program, Mr. Duncan? Is he really your uncle, Kaitlin?"

The other soccer players all gathered around the director and Kaitlin while he politely signed their programs. Sarah and her mom watched.

When he was finished with the autographs, Richard turned to them. "I'll call you in the morning, Sarah," he said. "We can all meet for lunch and discuss the details."

"That would be great," Sarah said. "Thank you so much and goodnight!"

"Where do you want to go to celebrate?" Mrs. Snow asked as they went to the dressing room so Sarah could change out of her costume.

Sarah shrugged. Then she laughed. "You choose – anywhere but The Sweet Shop, that is!"

Her mom laughed. "Let's go! We have a lot to celebrate!"